AUGUST IS FOR ACE

MOUNTAIN MEN OF MUSTANG MOUNTAIN

KACI ROSE

Book Cover By: Kelly Lambert-Greer

Editing By: Debbe @ **On The Page, Author and PA Services**

CHAPTER 1

ACE

"JUST WHAT DO you think you're doing, Ruby?" I ask. She's obviously up to no good judging by how often she's peeking over her shoulder while staring at my announcement bulletin board.

"I just have something to put up and don't you dare take it down, Ace Walker!" Ruby scolds me for something I haven't even done yet.

But my military training tells me that I'm not going to like whatever she is doing. I'm slightly distracted by the beautiful woman that walks in the door. I've never seen her before, so she isn't a local. It's not uncommon for people to pass through on their way from Yellowstone National Park to Glacier National Park or vice versa.

I take a better look at her, and she appears to be in her late twenties with dark blond hair that falls just past her shoulders and hazel eyes that sparkle with life. Her skin is a light golden tan, which seems to be from the sun she's been enjoying this summer. She wears a navy tank top with white shorts and sandals, which only makes her skin tone look deeper. She's carrying an olive-green backpack she is using for a purse.

She's not from around here. It's plainly obvious.

Ruby notices me staring at the woman and smirks before walking out the door. I can't help but smile as I watch the woman take a seat at the bar.

"What can I get you to drink?" I ask.

"I should just get a glass of water, but a glass of whiskey sounds more appealing. Do you have anything to eat here?" she asks.

I hand her a laminated menu, which is just a sheet of paper listing the few things that we have that are easy to whip up.

"Oh, the nachos and a glass of whiskey," she says as she hands me back the menu.

I pour the whiskey and set it down in front of her with a glass of water before returning to the kitchen to get the nachos going.

That's when I remember to go check what Ruby put on my bulletin board. I head out and grab a rag to wipe down a few tables as well, but it's clear as day that Ruby has made me the next mountain man of the month in her little scheme.

I rip the paper off the bulletin board, forgetting all about the tables I was going to wipe down and storm back behind the counter. Then I grab my phone and shoot out a quick text to Ruby.

> Me: Not Happening, Ruby.

I attach a picture of the flyer I tore off the board.

> Ruby: Too late and you better put that back up!

I'll worry about Ruby's wrath for taking the poster down some other time. Going back into the kitchen to get the woman's nachos, I serve them to her just as my phone goes off again.

I check it, expecting Ruby, but instead, it's my buddy Jonas.

> Jonas: Save the date, bro. Maddie and I are getting married on September 2nd.

> Me: Wouldn't miss it.

I'm happy for him. Although they didn't have the whole big wedding thing, they are doing it now with a real wedding in the works, and we'll get to celebrate them properly.

"So, mountain man of the month, huh?" The woman nods toward the flyer.

"The mayor's wife has been doing this to me and my buddies all year, no matter how much we protest and tell her to stop." I sigh and crumple the paper in my hand before tossing it in the trash.

"Well, Ace, I'm Everly and I'm pretty sure my dad

would do something like that to me given the chance. He keeps telling me to settle down, too."

The evening crowd starts to stumble in, and we talk in between customers. She's in town visiting her dad and is a vet. We don't get into personal details like who her dad is, but she tells me some crazy stories from her clinic back in Denver and I find I like this woman. She's smart and we can hold an actual conversation instead of talking about clothes and make-up.

As the last of the customers head out, she's still here talking to me, and I partly wonder if she wants to avoid seeing her dad. She has been openly flirting with me and switched to water two hours ago after nursing that one drink for over an hour.

"I don't normally do this, but I've enjoyed talking to you, and I have a place upstairs if you'd like to join me," I say. Then I cringe because it sounds like I'm trying to hook up with her instead of just not wanting to say goodbye.

"Yeah, I'd like that," she says with a smile, not even missing a beat.

"Okay, let me talk to the kitchen guy who's going to do clean up," I say.

I go and talk to Dan who helps out with the kitchen and also helps me close up.

"You okay to close up for me?" I ask him.

"Yeah, no problem. You taking that pretty blond home?" he winks.

Dan is a prior military officer like I am and in his late forties. A skinny guy who lives in a camper van on a piece of land he bought. He lives off the land and needs very little, so he's happy with a part-time job here. That's why we work well together.

I hate that he's referring to her as "that pretty blond" like she's just a piece of meat, but I let it go. That's just how he is. Dan's a good worker, and I don't need any bad blood between us.

"Something like that," I grumble and make sure the doors are locked before going back to Everly.

"Ready?" I ask. She stands and gathers her things before following me out back to the stairs.

"Do you make it a regular thing to follow guys out the back of the building in the middle of the night?" I ask as we head up the stairs.

"No, but many people came up to me tonight to sing your praises, so I feel safe enough."

"Joys of a small town," I grumble as I unlock the door.

"It's a nice change from the big city where you could be assaulted on the street, and everyone will ignore it and walk on by."

I stop to look at her, wondering if she knows that from experience, but she shakes her head.

"I read about it in the paper right before I left." She shrugs and sets her stuff down on the small round dining table as she takes a look around.

I have a cabin up on the mountain, but I use this space when I'm too tired to make the drive or when I close late and have to open early for inventory or events. I haven't brought anyone else up here before, though I doubt she'd believe that.

"All the more reason I love Mustang Mountain. I couldn't imagine living in the big city again," I say, grabbing a bottle of water from the fridge for each of us.

"Again?" she asks before taking a sip of hers.

"I was in the military before coming here. Mostly stationed in big cities. If my uncle hadn't left me the bar and the cabin when he died, I'm not sure what I would have done, but I know it wouldn't have been in the city."

We talk a bit more about how we both don't like the big city and how she wishes she could live in a town like Mustang Mountain, but her career just won't allow it until she has more practice under her belt.

We sit on the couch, each turned in so we can face each other. Her face is illuminated by the low lamplight and the soft light of the moon streaming in through the window. I can see every detail, from her full lips to her sparkling eyes that seem to be spinning with stars.

Her eyes light up as she talks about her work and what she does. I can tell how much she enjoys it. I feel the heat radiating off her body and a sudden urge to kiss her is so strong I can't resist it.

I hesitate for just a moment. But when her lips part slightly and her eyes drift to my lips, I know she is thinking of kissing me, too.

Before I can talk myself out of it, I lean forward and capture her lips with mine. She responds eagerly as she wraps her arms around my neck, drawing me closer until I am so close, I can feel her heart beating against me.

The kiss is electric, and I can feel my body responding as she presses her body closer to me. Deepening the kiss, I explore her mouth with my tongue until we are both breathless.

We break apart, just looking into each other's eyes before leaning in for another kiss that is even more passionate than the first.

I don't think a kiss has ever felt like this. Not just mind-blowing, but so perfect. Just the touch of her lips to mine has my cock hard. I've never been so damn turned on by just a kiss.

"You should stay here tonight. It will still be dark when you leave in the morning, so you won't have to worry about anyone seeing you," I whisper against her lips.

She tries to lean in for another kiss, but I pull back, waiting for an answer.

Her eyes focus on me, and she nods. "Okay."

Her words are barely out of her mouth before my lips are back on hers again.

We kiss hot and heavy, both of us getting more and more turned on with each passing second. I can feel her heart beating faster as our tongues intertwine and explore each other's mouths.

My hands drift down her back until they find the hem of her shirt. I slip my hands underneath and caress the soft skin of her back as we continue to kiss.

When we finally touch skin-to-skin, she gasps in pleasure.

Pulling away just enough to look her in the eye, I stand and offer her my hand. She takes it without hesitation as I lead her to the bedroom.

The room is dark, illuminated only by the light of the moon streaming in from the window. Stopping for a minute, I want to take in her beauty in the moonlight. I want to remember this moment forever, just us here together. Something to look back on with a smile.

The moment is broken when I feel her tugging at my shirt, pulling me closer as she slowly begins to undress me. I tense just a bit before taking her hands in mine and switch to undressing her first.

Her clothes fall to the floor, and once again I take a moment to admire her before sweeping her up into my arms and carrying her to the bed. Setting her down, I slowly undress, careful not to let her see my back before moving to the bed.

I lie down beside her and pull her close to me as we kiss again. This time there is something more, something deeper than before. I feel like I could get lost in this moment forever, just the two of us entwined together in a passionate embrace.

The kiss grows more intense with each passing second until finally I can't take it anymore and break away. We both gasp for air, our chests heaving as we look into each other's eyes.

She smiles at me, a look of pure joy on her face that sends my heart racing even faster than before.

I know what I want, and I can tell she does, too. Reaching over to the nightstand, I grab a condom and slide it on.

While I kiss every bit of skin I can reach, she thrusts her hips against my length. She is soaking wet. Even though I try to hold out as long as I can, she is driving me crazy with her soft moans.

Taking a breath, I look into her eyes before slowly thrusting into her. She cries out in pleasure, and I can feel the intensity of our connection grow even more as I thrust into her over and over again.

"Fuck sweetheart, I don't remember the last time I felt anything as good as you feel right now," I tell her.

She gets impossibly tighter, and I groan just trying not to give in to the threatening orgasm before she has a chance to cum.

Finally, she does, tightening around me and pushing me over the edge. I moan out her name as I cum, my body shaking with pleasure and satisfaction.

We lay there for a few moments, both of us panting and trying to catch our breath.

Getting up, I remove the condom and clean her up before pulling her into my arms, and she snuggles into me.

"Please tell me we can do that at least once more tonight," she says.

"Give me a bit to rest and we will definitely be doing that again," I chuckle.

Neither of us sleeps that night, and as the sun starts to rise, she gets out of bed.

"I should get going," she says, pulling her clothes on.

"As much as I'd love to say I want you to stay, it's probably best you leave before it gets too much later. People tend to talk here," I tell her.

She walks into the bathroom and while she's in there, I get dressed, starting with my shirt. Then I pull on my jeans, and I've just slipped on my leather jacket when she steps out of the bathroom.

Her gaze runs over my jacket, and then her eyes go wide.

"You're part of the Mustang Mountain Riders?" she says as she brushes a finger over my patch.

"Yes. Why?"

"Shit. I have to go." She gathers her things faster than I can register what is going on.

"What? Why?" I ask as her hand touches the door.

She doesn't even look back as she races out the door, slamming it behind her.

CHAPTER 2
EVERLY

I DID the one thing I swore to my dad I would never do. He made me promise years ago that I would never be with a guy from a motorcycle club. His exact words were he never wanted me to be with a man like him. He and Mom split up when I was young, and my mom moved with me and my brothers down to Denver. Back then, my dad got in and out of a lot of trouble.

When he finally settled down, he came to Denver. I was twelve the first time he visited, and he's been coming back to Denver every so often since then. This is my first time in Mustang Mountain, but my brothers remember it and have great things to say about it.

"Dad, I really think I should go to the clinic and get familiar with the setup and how they do things before tomorrow," I say. While I try to wrack my brain for any excuse to get out of this barbecue he's trying to take me to.

"We both know that someone is meeting you there tomorrow to give you the lay of the land, and they don't expect you in before then. Things are done differently around here. Besides, I've been talking you up to the guys, and I can't wait for you to meet them," Dad says, twisting the knife in my gut just a little bit more.

My dad's an old motorcycle guy through and through with a long gray beard and a bald head that he always has covered with a bandana or hat. He can look a bit scary if you don't know him. Growing up, he could give me one of his serious looks and I'd fall right into line.

Now, as an adult, I realize he's more of a teddy bear until you make him mad. And making him mad is the last thing I want, so he can never find out what happened with Ace.

I never do things as reckless as a one-night stand, but I thought maybe while I was here in Mustang Mountain, I could find someone to let loose with and have fun. Ace was fun to talk to and be around. So, when he and I clicked, I figured he would be that person. And man is he damn good in bed!

The problem came the next morning when I realized he was part of the Mustang Mountain Riders, just like my dad. And now Dad wants to take me to a barbecue at their clubhouse and show me off. The last thing I need is for everyone to know what happened between Ace and me.

I'm learning quickly that what you see on TV

about how everyone knows everybody in a small town, and how gossip travels fast, is true. My whole life I grew up in Denver and the chances of seeing someone you know walking down the street are so small that you have a better chance of being hit by a car crossing the road.

Here you have a better chance of running into someone you know than you do seeing a bird in the sky. In short, pretty much every time you step foot outside, someone is going to stop to talk to you.

Thankfully, my dad wasn't expecting me until this morning, so I didn't have to make up an excuse to say where I was last night. As far as I know, no one saw me leave the bar yesterday morning. So, I took a long drive around Mustang Mountain before heading to my dad's. Other than him being shocked I got in so early, he didn't to question it. Though I had to make up some excuse about getting too tired and resting at a hotel not too far from here. Once I arrived, he just got me set up in my room above the garage, made me breakfast, and let me take a shower. It's been nice to catch up with him, but this party is definitely too much.

Realizing I'm not going to get out of this cookout, I head upstairs and get ready. When I find myself standing in front of my mirror checking out my outfit and wondering if Ace would like it, I give myself a mental kick and go downstairs. Who cares if he likes it or not?

"I'm taking the bike and if you don't want to ride on

the back, you're more than welcome to take my truck. Plus, then you'll have a vehicle when you try to sneak out early, which I know you will." My dad hands me his truck keys, and I give him a grateful smile. He insisted on doing some minor work on my car before I drive it around town, so I don't have my car today.

I follow him to what he calls the clubhouse. There are a few cars parked out front, but mostly motorcycles fill the side yard of the building. He parks his and joins me at the truck before walking me inside.

"This place used to be a brothel back in the Wild West days. Sometime around the '80s, a family bought it. They wanted to turn it into a museum, but there just wasn't enough tourism in the area back then, and there was too much to fix up. So, we got it for a steal and have worked on renovating and trying to keep as much of its sordid history as we can." Dad offers a smile as we walk up the path to the door.

He opens the door for me and instantly the sound of music, laughter, and conversation that I couldn't hear from outside fill the air. I wasn't sure what to expect. The whole first floor is pretty open, with a large bar off to one side.

There are tables scattered around, with chairs and a dance floor on one side. It almost feels like walking into an Old West saloon, but with very modern people, electricity, and air conditioning.

I immediately start scanning the room for Ace, and when I find him at the far end of the bar staring at the door, his eyes are already on me. His face gives nothing away.

"Here, let me introduce you to a few of the guys whose girls I think you'll get along with," Dad says. I think he means men his age that have daughters my age, but I'm wrong.

"This is Ford and Luna, and you'll find their daughter Izzy running around somewhere. And this is Emma and Jackson." My dad introduces me to two couples that are about my age.

"This is my daughter Everly. She's a veterinarian and filling in at Dr. Thomas's clinic for the summer," Dad tells them proudly.

They welcome me with open arms and my dad introduces me to several more couples as we head to the bar to grab a drink. That's when we run into Ace.

"This is Ace Walker. He owns the bar in town and is one of the many military veterans here in the clubhouse." My dad shakes Ace's hand.

"This is my daughter Everly. She is in town for the summer." Then he turns to me. "You should go to his bar at some point. They've got some great live music and dancing and Ace makes one of the best burgers in town. Though if you tell Ruby I said that, I will completely deny it. Excuse me for a minute." Dad goes off to join a group of guys who are flagging him over, leaving me with Ace.

"Excuse me for the lack of decorum, but what the hell is going on here, sweetheart?" Ace asks.

My heart does this weird thing when he calls me

"sweetheart" but it's not anything special to a guy like him. He probably calls everyone sweetheart. It's what these guys do.

I'm thankful that my dad didn't give his whole "this is my daughter, the veterinarian" speech to Ace. The less he knows, probably the better.

"That's my dad, and that's why I freaked out when I saw your patch. No one can ever know what happened between us," I tell him.

"Your dad is an amazing guy and a great mentor to me. The last thing I would ever do would be to sleep with his daughter if I had known. So, I can promise you I'm not telling anyone. Are you really in town for the summer?" he asks, and his tone seems to soften.

"Yeah, it seemed like a good opportunity to visit my dad since he was always the one to visit me growing up."

"Can't imagine your dad in Denver, but I guess that explains why he's always cursing big cities," he says with a half-smile that I don't think he even realizes how sexy it is.

"He'd always rent a place just outside the city and he'd bring his truck, not his bike down. I'm sure that was partly my momma's doing."

"So, you're a veterinarian. Your dad talks about you all the time," Ace says.

"She's one of the youngest. Not only that, but she worked hard and took classes every summer so she could graduate early." My dad says as he walks up behind me and wraps an arm over my shoulders.

I never begrudge him the chance to brag about me, even as uncomfortable as it makes me. But right now, is one time I wish he wouldn't.

For the rest of the barbecue, Ace and I act like we just met and had no idea who each other was. I'm thankful that hopefully I can get out of this and forget it ever happened.

I'M at the bar today to do inventory and mostly to have something to do to keep my mind off Everly. The curvy blonde has set my entire world off balance, and I'll be damned if I don't seem to mind.

As I take a bag of trash out behind the bar, I'm trying to remember the brand of beer that Shaw and Owen asked me to get while we were at the cookout the other day. I'm so lost in my head that I trip over a box near the dumpster. I know I didn't leave it there.

Immediately, there are teeny tiny meows coming from the box, and I freeze. Praying I'm hearing things, I toss the trash into the dumpster, then lean down and open the box.

To my absolute horror, there are six of the smallest kittens I've ever seen in my life. They almost look like little blobs and their eyes aren't even open. Right then I know they're not even old enough to be away from their mother.

Some asshole dropped them here. You've got to be fucking kidding me. I reach for my phone and call Asher. He normally deals with large animals, but I he'll know what to do. The phone rings and I eventually land on his voicemail. Hanging up, I try again but get nothing.

I let out a few curse words even though I know that means he is probably out on a call. There's no telling how long this box has been here or how long these kittens have been away from their mother, and I know newborns need to eat often. Opening my phone, I try to find another veterinarian's office. There's one just outside of town, so I carefully pick up the box and say a prayer of thanks that I brought my truck instead of my bike today.

Gently placing the box on the leather seat of my truck, I get in. I look at the box and then reach over and wrap the seat belt around it just to be safe. Then I plug the address of the veterinarian's office into my GPS and head off.

I know absolutely nothing about cats. I've always been a dog person myself, so I have no idea what to do, but taking them to a vet seems like the right move. When I pull into the clinic, there's only one car in the parking lot and I hope that means there won't be a long line of people ahead of me. I grab the box and go inside. There's no receptionist at the front desk, and other than the sound of a dog barking from the back, it's relatively quiet.

"Hello?" I call out. Then there are sounds of someone walking on the tile floor coming toward me.

When Everly peeks around the corner of the wall, I probably could have been pushed over with a feather from shock.

"Ace? What are you doing here? I told you we can't do this anymore and if my dad sent you, then I really can't talk about this right now." She sighs and crosses her arms across her chest.

"Listen, I had no idea you worked here. I just found this box of kittens by the dumpster behind the bar. Their eyes aren't even open yet. Even though I know nothing about cats, I don't think they're old enough to be away from their mom, and I don't know what to do. My buddy Asher isn't picking up his phone. He was my first call since he works with animals." I'm rambling because I feel a sense of urgency to get these animals looked at to make sure they're okay.

She looks at the box and bites her lip before coming forward and opening it. Her eyes go wide, then she looks up at me.

"Come with me." She turns and walks to the back of the clinic without even looking to see if I'm following. Instead of taking me to an exam room, we go to the back of the clinic where there's a metal exam table, one that looks like they might use it for surgery.

"Set the box on the table so I can get a look at them, please." She nods toward the metal exam table then starts pulling things out of cabinets and setting them on the counter before she washes her hands.

"How long ago did you find them?" she asks as she pulls the first kitten from the box.

"About twenty minutes ago. As soon as Asher didn't pick up his phone, I brought them straight here."

"Any idea how long they've been out there?" she asks, setting the gray one down and picking up another one.

"No, that was the first time I'd been out there this morning and I had parked out front. I know they weren't there last night because I was the one to take the trash out and lock the door. That was at about one o'clock."

"We need to feed them now, and I'm going to need help because I don't have anyone here." She looks up at me.

"I don't like cats, and I was kind of hoping to just bring them here and let the vet take care of them," I say, taking a step back.

"If these guys don't eat and soon, they're going to die. There's already a good chance that half of them may not even make it through the night. I need help. I'm filling in for this vet over the summer and no one is going to be here until tomorrow. Though I wouldn't even know who to call for help, anyway." She sets another kitten back into the box before turning around to the cabinet behind her and pulling out what looks like a small dog bed. She sets it on the table, then slowly starts pulling the kittens out of the box and placing them on the pet bed.

The military drilled into me that we leave no man

behind, and it's a personal motto I abide by. I don't abandon anyone who needs help because I know what that helplessness feels like.

"Okay, just tell me what to do."

"First, go wash your hands as I get the food set up."

I walk over to the sink where she washed her hands earlier and scrub mine down with soap and water. When I turn around, she's pulled out six tiny bottles that look like they're for dolls, not animals, and she's filling them up with what looks like milk but has some fancy doctor label on it.

She then turns and arranges the cats so they're all facing one way.

"You take the three on that side. I'll take the three on this side. We need to get them to latch on and nurse from the bottle. Watch me."

She picks up the bottle and starts with the first cat. Tilting the bottle upside down until there's just a tiny bit of milk on the tip of the bottle, she then rubs it against the cat's mouth. The cat immediately starts moving and within a moment, is latched onto the bottle. She holds it in one hand and then does the same to the next cat. Once that one latches on, she's able to hold the two bottles in one hand while she gets the third cat set up.

I start with my three and do the same. It takes a little bit, but all three of them latch and start feeding. When I look over at her, she has a concerned look on her face.

"What's wrong?" I ask.

"My third one here isn't latching."

Looking down, I find one of the little gray kittens fast asleep with no interest in the bottle, even as Everly runs it across the front of its nose.

"So, what do we do now?" I ask her.

"I need to feed it with a syringe once these guys are done."

Slowly I shift the bottles of the ones that I'm feeding into one of my hands. These guys are so tiny, and the bottles aren't much bigger, so I'm able to hold three of the bottles in one of my big hands. I reach across and gently take the two bottles she's holding in the other hand. The position isn't exactly the most comfortable, but she needs to focus on the one that's not eating.

"Do what you have to do," I tell her.

She hesitates for a moment and looks at me before she nods and goes into the cabinet coming back with a syringe. She opens the lid of the bottle and sucks the milk into the syringe. When she's done with that, she gently picks up the cat and wraps a washcloth around it. Then she slowly tries to feed the kitten.

"He's very lethargic. His movements are really slow, almost like he doesn't have the energy to swallow the milk that I place on his tongue." She cradles him up to her chest and rubs him all over as she walks over to another cabinet and pulls a blanket out.

She wraps the kitten in the blanket and continues

to rub it as she walks around opening cabinets like she's looking for something. Finally, she pulls out another syringe. This one has a small tube attached to the end.

"If I can get the milk down his throat, he just has to swallow it. Once they are done eating, you need to rub their back and belly to stimulate them to pee. They won't do it on their own yet. There are towels in the cabinet behind you, I think."

Sure enough, towels are right where she said they would be.

"You seem to know this place pretty good for someone who's just filling in." I grab a couple of towels and pick up the first kitten to do as she said.

"I've been here for a few hours, and all I've been doing is trying to figure out where everything is."

I watch her try to get the kitten to eat as I get each of the other kittens to pee before settling them down and seeing them fall asleep.

"Is he getting any of the milk?" I ask, but she just shakes her head.

"Not enough. There's a good chance he won't make it through the night. Unfortunately, there's a chance none of them are going to make it through the night, because I can't manage all of them on my own.

"There's no one coming in today to help?" I ask, glancing at my watch to see it's only eleven in the morning.

"No, the clinic is normally closed today."

"Let me make a few calls to get someone to cover the bar, and I'll stay and help."

"You don't have to do that," she says in protest.

"It's already done."

Besides, if she thinks I'm passing up this chance to spend more time with her, she's out of her mind.

THE CATS ARE ALL FINALLY asleep after being fed and using the restroom, all except the gray one who's been giving me problems. He's holding on, so there's still a chance he'll make it.

"Are you hungry? I can head down to the cafe and get us some lunch," Ace says.

I'm about to tell him I'm fine, but my stomach rumbles giving away the fact that I skipped breakfast too. I go to my purse to give him some money. "Actually, lunch sounds pretty good. I could go for a BLT and some French fries if they have it."

"I'm buying. I think it's the least I can do after disrupting all your plans for the day with these cats. And they do have a BLT with herbed mayo. It's a town favorite. Lock the door behind me. I'll be back shortly."

After locking the door behind him, I go back and start making a list of all the supplies we used. Then I make another list of what we're going to need to take care of the kittens. Hopefully, tomorrow when the receptionist gets in, she'll know how to order them. I was told that she knows how to run the entire place, so I'm assuming she will.

There's a knock at the front door, and as I peek around the corner through the large double glass doors, I can see Ace standing there with bags of food and a tray of drinks. Letting him in, I grab the tray of drinks and lead the way back to the area where the kittens are.

"They slept the whole time. I think we have enough time to eat before they'll need to be fed again," I say as we set the food on a small desk off to the side.

"So, tell me about yourself, Ace. Other than bar owner, mountain man of the month, kitten rescuer, and Mustang Mountain Rider, who are you?" I ask out of pure curiosity. The question seems to make him uncomfortable.

"I'm sorry. You don't have to answer. I was just trying to start some small talk," I tell him, wishing now that I hadn't asked because I don't want to make him uncomfortable. I really do need his help.

"No, it's fine. I just haven't had to talk about myself for a while. It's not a pretty story, sweetheart. My dad left when I was young, and I was raised by a single mom. We didn't have very many options, so I went into the military after high school. A year later, my mom died while I was on deployment. Had a couple of girl-friends that didn't work out. After one particularly hard deployment, I found out that my uncle who I hadn't heard from since I was about ten, died and left me his cabin and bar here in Mustang Mountain. It was perfect timing, so I came out here and I haven't left."

My stepdad insisted I take at least one psychology elective in school just so I could understand body language and cues since as a vet I was going to have to rely on the animal's human to figure out what was going on. I wasn't thrilled about the idea, but I'm so thankful that he did because those skills have come in handy. Like now, I can tell Ace is leaving out some important details, but I also know I'm in no position to push for them.

"Now it's your turn. I'm happy to answer questions, but you're going to have to answer the same ones."

"Oh, well, I'm the youngest. I've got two older brothers from my mom's first marriage. Then my mom and my dad got together, but I guess my dad wasn't in a good place at the time. They lived here in Mustang Mountain for a while, and I was born here, but I don't remember it. We moved to Denver when I was three, and I was ten when Mom married my stepdad. My brothers all remember the area and have great things to say about it, but this is the first time I'm here to see it. My dad helped set up this job so that I could spend some time with him, see the area, and decide if my own practice is what I really want."

"Is it?" he asks.

"That's always been the dream, because why become a vet to work for someone else? But I'll tell you something I haven't told my parents, I hate living in

Denver. I don't like big cities. They make me nervous and anxious, and I'm constantly looking over my shoulder. This is my chance to see if I can hack it in a small town, too. That's why I took the job." My cheeks flush, but it feels so good to admit it to someone.

Just then, we hear the front door close, but no one calls out or says anything.

"Stay here," Ace says, but I don't listen and follow him right out front. If someone has an animal emergency, I need to be there.

Instead, there's this guy with a gray hoodie on and jeans that have a lot of dirt stains on them. He's looking around, and my gut says he's not up to anything good.

"Can I help you?" Ace asks, standing there at his full height and crossing his arms. He's well over six feet tall and looks quite intimidating. The guy glances up and stumbles back a few steps when he sees Ace.

"No... I was... um... looking..." The guy keeps stumbling over his words like he's trying to think of an excuse, but his brain isn't keeping up.

"You were just looking to leave. Now. Don't bother coming back in here, either," Ace says, his tone scary.

The guy scrambles out the door, and Ace follows him, locking it right behind him.

"You could have at least let him spit out what he was going to say. Even if he was trying to make an excuse, we need to make sure he didn't actually have an animal that needed help," I scolded him a bit.

"That guy was up to no good," he says as we return to the back room.

"You don't know that."

"Listen, sweetheart, you'll never get an argument from me about Mustang Mountain being safer than Denver, but we're not without our problems, either. He looked like he was casing the place, and we've had a string of burglaries recently. It happens now and then. It's usually someone passing through who sees us as an easy target. And you're probably not going to like what I have to say next," he says as he pulls out his phone.

"And what would that be?"

"I'm going to have to call your dad and tell him. If that guy has any idea that the vet is out of town or that a single woman is running the place, we need to make sure we have a few extra eyes on you," he says. Before I can even protest, he has the phone up to his ear.

Great, my one chance to prove to my dad that I can take care of myself, and Ace is already running to him on my behalf for help. Once it starts ringing, at least he puts the phone on speaker so I can hear what's going on.

"Hey, Ace. How's it going?" My dad asks.

"Well, sir, we've got a bit of a problem, but let me explain," he says, looking at me.

"There's no problem. You're overreacting." I sigh and sit down to finish my lunch.

"Is that Everly?" My dad asks.

"Yes, I'm here with her at the clinic. I found some kittens that were abandoned by my dumpster and when Asher didn't answer his phone, I brought them here. I didn't realize this was where she was working.

But that's not the problem. You've heard about the string of break-ins we've had recently, right?"

"Yes, is she okay?" My dad's tone suddenly sounds serious.

"I'm fine, Dad," I say, glaring at Ace once again.

"She's fine, but we just had a guy step in, and he was shady as hell, dirty, sketchy, and looked like he was casing the place. If they're robbing places for drugs and heard the vet was out of town, maybe they thought they could get in here and get their hands on some. I scared him off. That doesn't mean he won't be back, though."

"When people on drugs start to hit rock bottom and get desperate, they aren't thinking straight. They're also very unpredictable. Sadly, I've seen it firsthand. I think it's best we have someone there with her while she's at the clinic, at least until we catch whoever's behind these burglaries or track down the guy you saw." My dad jumps on Ace's crazy bandwagon.

"Guys, I'm fine. I'll keep the door locked when I'm here, and after today I'll very rarely be here alone."

"Not good enough," Ace says.

At the same time, my dad says no way.

"That isn't all," Ace says, catching our attention.

"What is it?" My dad asks.

"He had a Savage Bones Tattoo on his arm," Ace says.

I slump into my chair, knowing that I'm not going to win this argument. I have no idea who the Savage

Bones are, but I can tell it's not good by the string of curses my dad lets out.

"I can arrange for some of the guys to be here and help keep an eye on things," Ace tells my dad.

"Sounds good. I can fill in a few days myself. Just let me know."

They say their goodbyes and hang up as Ace looks over at me.

"I don't need a bunch of babysitters, you know," I tell him as I finish my lunch.

"Not a bunch, just me. I know you don't, but I'd rather keep you safe." He sits down and starts on his food again.

"What do you mean, just you?"

"The clinic is open when the bar is closed. Most of my friends are married or settled with their girlfriends now. They can fill in every so often, but asking them to do a regular rotation... it's a bit too much. So, you're stuck with me."

"Great. Who are the Savage Bones?"

"They're another MC club, a one-percent club."

"What's a one-percent club?" I ask as I finish up my fries.

"A long time ago, the American Motorcycle Association said ninety-nine percent of motorcycle clubs operate within the law. After that, some clubs started calling themselves the one percent. They brag about being outside the law. Basically, they're the drug dealers and the guys who work in the arms trade and the sex trade, willingly and unwillingly."

"So, these Savage Bones guys aren't good people," I say, trying to wrap my head around what Ace just told me.

"Nope, and they've been trying to push their way into Mustang Mountain and the surrounding areas. We won't let them, but it's an uphill fight."

"So that tattoo means he's part of the other club?"

"He is, or he used to be. It takes a lot to get thrown out of those clubs. So if he is a past member, he's even more dangerous," Ace says.

I'm saved from thinking too much about it as the kittens start to stir. I get up to make another batch of milk so we can feed them again. Ace scarfs down his food and takes the bottles I've prepared over to the kittens.

I get the syringe ready for the little guy who didn't want to eat last time. He's still not as active as his siblings, but he's more energetic this time. As I get some of the milk down the back of his throat, he swallows it.

"How's he doing?" Ace asks, nodding to the little guy in my hands.

"He's finally drinking some milk, but he only took about half of what his siblings did. I'm going to try to get him to go potty, but I don't think he's had enough fluids to do so." I rub him in a blanket to try to stimulate him to urinate.

After checking the towel, there are only a few tiny drops which is better than nothing. It means at least his organs are still functioning. Setting him down, I help stimulate the others as they finish eating. Once they're back asleep, I take all of our dirty towels to the back and get a load of laundry going. Thankfully, they have a washer and dryer here in the office.

"I'm going to call Ruby. She should have an idea if anyone can take care of a few cats. Then she could start making some phone calls for us," he says, pulling out his phone.

"Who's Ruby?" I ask, thinking maybe it's his wife or girlfriend, and he's just like every other guy.

"She's the mayor's wife and the queen of the gossip tree. Not only does she know everyone and everything, she can spread gossip faster than wildfire," he says with a smile on his face. "She's also the one who put the mountain man of the month poster up that night at the bar."

I remember an older woman leaving as I walked in, but I couldn't pick her out of a crowd if I tried.

"Hey Ruby, I need a favor." He talks into the phone, but I can't hear what Ruby is saying.

"No, I'm not putting that damn poster back up, but this is more serious than whether or not you can pimp me out for the month." He sounds irritated, and honestly, it's kind of cute.

"Someone abandoned a box of kittens behind the bar that aren't even a week old. I'm at the vet with them now, but they need around-the-clock care. I was wondering if you know of anyone who could take in one or two of them to do feedings and help out." He pauses and almost rolls his eyes.

"Yes, I can call the guys, but I wanted to see if you

know anyone who has any experience with cats first. You know the guys will have no clue what they're doing."

"Okay well, text me who I should be looking for. I'm here at the clinic now." He pauses for a moment and then shakes his head.

"No, not Asher. I couldn't get a hold of him. Yeah, that's the one."

He hangs up and smiles over at me.

"She's going to make a few calls and see if she can get some people down here to help. Once we know who she can muster up, I'll call some of the guys with the MC. I know I can pull their girls' heartstrings and they'll each take on a cat."

He helps me clean up the place and we go through another feeding before his phone rings again. This time he places it on speakerphone as he finishes drying the bottles that we just used for the feeding.

"Hey, Ruby," he answers.

"So, I made a few calls and the girls that I had in mind are all on vacation and out of town. I was able to get one who can take one of the kittens, but I'm still working on the others. Her name is Jackie, and she'll be in later this afternoon," Ruby says.

"Okay, perfect. I'll call and see if I can twist some of the guys' arms to get them to take a few as well."

"How many do we have in total?" Ruby asks.

It doesn't escape me that after just one call this seems to be her fight too. That simple question of how many kittens *we* have shows me that I'm worlds away from Denver.

Ace walks into the front office area, starts making some phone calls, and a few hours later, there's a group of people standing in the front office. Five couples are standing there along with Jackie. It's feeding time so Ace and I show them on the one kitten how to go about mixing the food, how to feed them, and how I've been using a syringe. I answer any questions, and then I pull out the paperwork to start keeping track of where each cat goes.

"Can we take the mostly black one, Daddy? Please, please, please, please?" A little girl who I hadn't noticed before asks.

"Izzy, you'd better ask Luna if she's up for the challenge. If she is, then you can pick which cat we take," one of the men says.

"That's Ford and Luna, and their daughter, Izzy," Ace says from beside me.

"That's fine. We need to talk to the vet and make sure we know everything we'll need to take care of him," Ford says.

They come up to pick up the kitten, and I hand them a little bag Ace helped me put together that holds everything they'll need for the next few days.

"What's his name?" the little girl asks me.

"He doesn't have one, so you'll be able to give him a name and let us know what it is so we can write it down," I tell her. She lights up with a huge smile as they head out.

"Really, Ace? You had to call Emma before you talked to me?" A tall guy with broad shoulders comes up next.

"We all know you would have said no, and they need help," the blonde woman with him says.

"This is Jackson and Emma." Ace introduces us as Emma snuggles one of the kittens against her chest.

"Is this what you were trying to call me about earlier?" Another guy walks up with a woman next to him.

"Yeah, when I couldn't get ahold of you, I came here. Everly, this is Asher and Jenna. Asher runs the mustang refuge in town. He's a vet as well, but mostly works with large animals."

We chat for a moment before they pick up the little kitten I'd been feeding with a syringe along with another one of the smaller kittens. Since he's a vet, I'm not worried about him taking two.

"Well, since the others are chit-chatting, let me see which of these guys is left." Jackie comes up with a huge smile on her face.

She looks at the two kittens left and runs her hand over each of them. One seems to snuggle up against her hand more than the other.

"I think this little one is going to come home with me. She's perfect with her gray stripes and all," she says, picking her up and grabbing the bag to go with her.

The next couple steps up behind Jackie.

"This is Jensen and his girl, Courtney," Ace says.

They take the last kitten along with the bag of supplies and leave.

Ace sticks around and helps me get the place clean and ready for the next day.

"I'll see you tomorrow. I promise I'll stay in the parking lot out of your way, but I'll be there if you need me." He walks me to my car, and I figure at this point it'll be useless to argue.

When he sits there bored all day and nothing happens, maybe he'll decide that it's just a big waste of time and move on.

I'VE BEEN at the vet's office watching over Everly every day this week. If anyone's watching the place, I've been switching up whether I bring my bike or my truck just so they don't see the same vehicle every day. Today, I rode my bike and was able to park so it's not seen from the street, but I still have a clear shot of the front door.

Thankfully, it's been relatively quiet, with no sign of the man in the hoodie that I saw the other day. There's some noise to my right, and I look over and find Hades rounding the building and coming over to sit next to me.

"Hey there, big guy. You've been keeping an eye on the place, too?" I pet him and dig into my pocket to give to him some of the trail mix I was munching on.

I've been watching some storm clouds rolling in all day and the first drops of rain start to pelt against my leather jacket.

"Figures the one day they say there's no rain, and I bring my bike, there actually is rain. But when they claim there's going to be rain, there isn't."

After I give him a little more trail mix, he turns around and goes back behind the building. He's probably off to be with Persephone, who's caring for their puppies during the storm. Mack says that Hades has been very protective of her.

It's raining pretty good now, but I just stand there and watch the door. The parking lot is mostly empty, but that doesn't mean I get to let my guard down. After taking another look down the street, the front door opens, and Everly steps out.

She looks as beautiful as ever, with her hair in a braid over her shoulder and her white lab coat on.

"If you're going to insist on staying here, at least come in out of the rain. Let's get you dry," she says with a sigh. She holds the door open for me as I follow.

"Due to the rain, I've had a couple of cancellations. No one wants to go out in this, and I can't blame them. Hang up your jacket and come sit in front of the heater in the back. Let's get you warmed up. I'm going to send the receptionist home. Since you're here, there's no point in keeping her when there are no more patients for the rest of the day." She leads me up front, pulls a chair up in front of the heater, and takes off my shoes.

A few minutes later she returns and starts pulling some items out of a box that I saw the mailman drop off earlier.

"I locked the front door, and it's just us in here, but

I'd like to stay for a little bit just to make sure there are no emergency calls from the storm. I don't know how it is here, but we always had several of them in Denver. I'm not sure what to expect."

"Well, I'm not going into the bar tonight. I have someone covering me, so I'm here for as long as you are," I tell her just as the power flickers then goes out.

"Great. Just what I need. Let me find you a clean blanket from the back. It will probably be best if you strip off your shirt and pants at the very least. Now that the heater is out, they can't be too comfortable."

I had no intention of removing my clothes, no matter how uncomfortable they were. At least in front of the heater they would dry. But with the power out, that's a different story. Maybe if I keep my back against the wall, or if she finds a blanket, I can keep over me if I'm cold, it won't be such a big deal.

She comes back with a large blanket and hands it to me without a word. Going to the bathroom, I step out of my clothes, and wrap the blanket over my back and shoulders. Thankfully, it's long enough that it covers me almost to the top of my knees. I take my wet clothes out in one hand and hold the blanket closed in the other.

Takings the clothes from me, she hangs them up as I sit in the chair I was sitting on before the power went out. I'm guessing they have a small backup generator because a few small lights are on, and one of their refrigerators is still going. It's the one that I remember her grabbing formula and some medicine from. Thankfully, it's still the middle of the day, so the light coming in from the windows keeps the place well lit.

We sit and talk for a while, and every so often she gets up to check and make sure the refrigerator with all the medication is still running. This time, on her way back, she walks behind me.

"What happened here?" she asks, touching the top center of my right shoulder blade. I hadn't even realized the blanket had dipped down.

I freeze and get pissed at myself for getting so comfortable that I didn't even realize the blanket had slipped. People always treat me differently after they see my scars, and I was enjoying my time around Everly.

"I was injured on deployment right before the military discharged me. I spent some time at Oakside Rehabilitation Center, which is when I found out about my uncle leaving me his place."

I tell her the shortened version. She doesn't need all the nasty details. And she doesn't need my sob story, but this should be enough to stop most of her questions.

Instead of moving away, she gently pulls the blanket further down my back. I should move away, but a voice in my head is telling me to let her see them and let her run now before I get too involved.

Who am I kidding, though? I'm already too involved with her, even if she isn't on board with it yet. It's still going to hurt like hell for her to pull away from me, but better now than later. She traces each of the scars with her fingertip.

"Why do you hide them?" she asks innocently as she continues to trace the largest one.

"Maybe we need to get you some glasses if you can't see how nasty they are." I try to joke with her. At the same time I try to pull the blanket back over them, but she doesn't let me.

"I see them just fine, and I don't see them as anything to hide."

"My ex thought they were. She dumped me because they were too ugly to look at." I finally tell her about the girl I had waiting on me when I came home from deployment—the one who didn't stick around.

"Well, she's an idiot and not all girls think like her. The people that do think like her? Fuck them."

I sit there, completely stunned. Not just by what she said, but by the dirty word that just came out of her beautiful mouth. I reach around and wrap a hand around one of her wrists and pull her around in front of me and onto my lap.

Her eyes meet mine and I'm frozen, waiting to see her next move. She doesn't hesitate as she leans in and kisses me. Fuck, does she taste good. Her lips are so soft and warm. I wrap my arms around her and hold on tight as she wraps her arms around my neck.

Without breaking the kiss, she removes the lab coat that she has on, and it drops to the floor. She shifts in my lap so that she's straddling me. I'm already hard and only in my boxer briefs, so there's no hiding it. The fabric of her black pants is so thin that I can feel how wet she is through our clothes, and I can't stand it.

I kiss her harder, focusing on the kiss and not anywhere else until she starts grinding on me.

"Fuck that feels good. I was trying to keep my distance from you. I tried and failed. If we do this, this time. You. Are. Mine. I don't care that your dad is one of my MC members. I don't care that you're in town temporarily. We'll figure it all out." I kiss her again.

"I don't have any answers for you. I just know I want you, and I want us to figure it out." She moves away just enough to speak.

I pull her back in and kiss her again. Her soft moans fill the air as she grinds against me harder and faster until I can't take it anymore. I move my hands over her luscious body.

I can feel every curve, every delicious inch as I explore with my hands. My lips make their way down her neck, trailing kisses until they reach the top of her shirt.

Slowly I unbutton her shirt until I can see all of her beautiful skin, and then I take a second to appreciate the view before moving on. My lips continue their journey from one side of her chest to the other, taking their time as they explore every inch of skin that they can find.

Frantic to feel each other without clothes in the way, we remove them quickly. Then she settles back on my lap.

The sensations that come with her being on me are

out of this world. I can feel myself getting closer and closer to the edge. I don't want to wait any longer, so I grip her hips and move her until I am lined up at her entrance.

She looks down at me with a look of pure pleasure, and I can barely contain myself. With one swift thrust, she is fully seated on me, and I let out a moan that rivals hers. We both move in perfect unison as we find our rhythm.

Her eyes are locked on mine, and all I can do is stare at her in awe. The pleasure that I'm feeling is almost unbearable, and I can tell she is close, too. But more than that, it's the intense connection between us.

With a few more thrusts, I feel her tense around me. Her screams of pleasure fill the room as I follow her over the edge.

We both collapse together as we catch our breath, and I'm reminded why I wanted to keep my distance in the first place. She is truly an amazing woman, and I can't wait to see what the future holds for us.

CHAPTER 6
EVERLY

THE CLINIC IS CLOSED TODAY, so Ace volunteered to show me around Mustang Mountain. Since my dad was busy, I agreed. We decided to meet at the MC Club, and boy am I glad I wore jeans today. It was a fashion choice and not because I was almost out of laundry.

"I didn't think you meant on the back of your bike when you suggested a tour of the area," I say when he pulls up.

"There are only a few months out of the year when it's comfortable to ride, so I take advantage of any time I can. Plus, it's the best way to take in the mountain." He hands me an extra helmet.

Taking it, I strap it on hesitantly. He leans over while still on the bike and tightens the straps before taking my hand and helping me onto the bike behind him.

I know how this goes. I'm supposed to hold on to

him. Though I can't lie and say I haven't thought about riding with him, wrapping my arms around him, and having an excuse to be that close to him. So, taking a deep breath, I swing one leg over the bike and sit behind him.

When I hesitate to wrap my arms around him, he seems to know I need that little push. He takes one of my hands and pulls it around to rest on his chest. Pulling me in even closer to him.

"Hold on tight, sweetheart," he says in his deep voice as he revs the engine.

I settle in, wrapping my arms around him and holding tight as he takes off out of the parking lot of the MC Club. He expertly navigates down the side roads to get us to the main road, where we head into town with the mountains to our backs.

Just as we can see the town ahead of us, he pulls into a park on our right. He slowly circles the parking lot before stopping.

"This is where we have a lot of town events. It's also part of what convinced me to stick around. I don't think I have ever found a place so calming, even in a large crowd," he says.

I look around him to find a beautiful city park situated around the cascading mountain views. I'm pretty sure my jaw falls open.

"You know, I don't think I've ever seen anything so beautiful," I say, my eyes on the view in front of us.

"I have," he says. When I glance over at him, he's looking back at me.

I swear if it weren't for these bulky helmets, he would have kissed me. Clearing my throat, I try to break the moment and get both of us to refocus.

"Show me what else Mustang Mountain has to offer," I say as we get going again.

We drive down the main street and several side streets where he shows me the town's hidden gems, like the beautiful historic train station. I also notice the town has benches placed in perfect spots to take in the views. A family of four sits on one while enjoying their ice cream cones. A couple sits on another, just snuggling up to people watch.

Finally, he goes back up Main Street with the mountain in front of us. The town looks like something from a postcard or some holiday small-town movie. We stop at the café and get a takeout order that we take to the park to eat. He pulls a blanket from the storage area under my seat, like he had this all planned.

We walk up from the parking lot and he lays the blanket down under a large tree. Then he puts the food down as we get settled. We both got sandwiches and fries, easy picnic food.

"So, your dad lives here, but you live with your mom in Denver. What made you decide to spend a summer here other than the vet job?" he asks as we start eating.

"I don't remember Mustang Mountain from when I was little. I know the stories and I've seen the photos. But the way my brothers describe the place, it seemed like this mystical fairyland when I was growing up. As my brothers got older, I asked them why they never moved back here. They said because our mom was in Denver and my dad's not their father, so it didn't make sense to, but they wished they could."

Then I stop, feeling like I overshared. I don't normally talk so much about my past.

"I visited Mustang Mountain when I was a kid too. Not anything that I remember, but my mom told me stories before she died. My uncle was my mom's brother. He never had kids, so when he died, he left everything to me. The timing was just right, and here I am. I just never left, and with each passing day, I have less and less of a desire to leave."

We talk more about our childhoods, growing up, and our parents. As we finish our lunch, he sets the boxes that our food came in aside and lays down on the blanket, pulling me down with him. I use his shoulder as a pillow, and we lie there under the shade of the big tree, breathing the fresh Montana air, and enjoying each other's company and conversation along with the stunning views.

I dated in high school and some more in college. I had some interesting first dates, and I've had guys try to impress me. They did things like setting up fancy events or experiences, concert tickets with front-row seats, fancy expensive restaurants, and the works.

Yet somehow, that all pales in comparison to lying here talking to Ace after a super simple picnic in the town park. I think what was missing in all those dates was a connection. There was no spark or rapport with those guys. Not like what Ace and I have.

I try to just enjoy myself and not think about what that means because if I think too hard my mind starts spinning. I'm only here temporarily, so where does that leave us?

AFTER THE AMAZING day I spent with Everly, showing her around town and then having lunch in the park, I know what I must do. I have to do things right and try to push away any fears that she might have.

So, stepping up onto the front porch in front of me, I knock on the large wooden door. I can hear voices on the other side, but it takes a minute before someone answers. The entire time my anxiety is ramping up. I don't remember the last time I've been this nervous to do anything except ask out my prom date. She only went with me to get back at her ex-boyfriend, who she was back together with by the third song of the night.

When the door opens, I'm standing face-to-face with Everly's dad.

"Is my daughter okay?" he asks, his face stone-cold serious.

"She's perfectly fine. I was hoping to talk to you

about something," I tell him as I shift my weight, not able to hold still.

He looks me over, then nods and opens the door for me to follow him inside.

"Head on into my office. Let me tell my old lady you're here," he says.

Since I've been to his house several times, I know my way down the hall to his office. I take the seat in one of the chairs. A moment later, he joins me, closing the door behind him, so I know we won't be disturbed.

"Are you sure Everly is, okay?" he asks again as he sits down across from me.

"Yes, she's okay, but I am here to talk to you about her," I tell him honestly.

He looks me over for a minute, but doesn't say anything right away.

"I'm listening," he says when he finally speaks.

I take a deep breath and start the speech I stayed up practicing all night.

"I don't know what she's told you, but we met before that cookout. When she first arrived, she came into the bar to grab a bite to eat. We got to talking, but I had no idea who she was. When she saw my patch, she fled. When I showed up with the kittens, I had no idea that was the vet office where she was working. I couldn't get ahold of Asher, and that was the next closest office."

"She told me about the kittens and how you stayed to help her with them. She filled in the details around our call." He nods, and I hope he's not reading in between the lines about what I'm leaving out. That's not something I want to talk to her father about.

"Well, we got to know each other and talked about our lives quite a bit. Then after that, I was sticking around and watching the clinic. During that big storm, they lost power, and we hung out then too, and shared about our dreams, plans and that sort of thing. She's easy to talk to. I don't open up a lot, but I find myself wanting to tell her things that I've had no desire to talk about before. Talking about her passion for the animals and their owners, being here and getting to know you, her eyes light up."

I pause, hesitating when her father leans back in his chair and crosses his arms over his chest. As I'm gushing about his daughter, I'm guessing he put two and two together and knows where I'm trying to go with this. So, there's no point beating around the bush.

"Your daughter is an amazing woman, and I would be honored to have the chance to get to know her more. But you're also my friend and I want to make sure I do this the right way, so I'm asking for your permission to date your daughter," I blurt out.

"You do understand that her being in Mustang Mountain is just temporary, right?" he says with his voice completely void of emotion.

"I know. But the way I feel about her? I'm going to do everything I can to get her to stay. Because I love her, and if it were up to me, I would marry her tomorrow. I know she's not ready for that. I'm willing to go at her pace and wait until she is ready. But that does include making her fall in love with Mustang Mountain and hopefully wanting to stay here."

There's just a glimmer in his eyes, and I know he likes the idea. Based on our previous conversations, he would love to have his daughter close where they can have a real relationship—more than just a long-distance one. Other than that glimmer in his eyes, there's no emotion on his face.

"And if she says she doesn't want to stay here?"

I've thought about this too, and it's a hard pill to swallow. While I know I can't say that I want her and that I love her, but expect her to move here and uproot her life if I'm not willing to do the same. I hate the idea of giving up the bar and my peace and quiet on the mountain here in Mustang Mountain to move to Denver. But the more I thought about it, I hated the idea of losing her more.

"I can't ask her to do something I wouldn't be willing to do myself. That's a code I lived by in the military, and one I still live by today. So, if she was adamant about not wanting to live here, but she still wanted me? I'd move to Denver."

He stares at me for just a moment longer before a full-blown smile takes over his face.

"Good. That's the best part of a relationship: you can't ask your partner to do something you aren't willing to do yourself. I've learned that one the hard way, and I wish I had known that with her mother. Things would have ended up a lot differently. I'm not the same person I was back then." He stares at the wall behind me, a far-off gaze in his eyes before they snap back to me.

"I would be honored to have you dating my daughter and eventually becoming my son-in-law. You're a good guy, but ultimately this is her choice and whatever her choice is, I will support her. So don't think just because you have my blessing, you can use that as a weapon against her."

He levels me with a serious look, and I wonder if it's because of something that has happened to her in the past or something that he has done in his past. Either way, I know better. I knew I could be the best of friends with her dad, and there's still the greatest chance she will shoot me down. But I have to try.

"I understand and just because she says no, it doesn't mean that I'm going to back away because I know what I want. If she's not ready now, I'll wait until she is." I lay all my cards on the table.

"Well, why don't you stay for dinner and let me get to know you a bit better? My old lady is always cooking too much food anyway and then trying to force it down my throat as leftovers for the rest of the week." He laughs as he stands up.

"I'd enjoy that. Home-cooked meals aren't a regular thing at the bar, as you can imagine."

One of the biggest hurdles—knowing I'm not going

to lose a friend or cause a ripple of issues at the club—
has been tackled. But I think the issue of getting her to
agree to be mine is just as big of a hurdle.

I'm not backing down. Whatever it takes, Everly
will be mine.

I'M HAVING dinner with my dad and his wife today. I have nothing against her. She's nice, but they got married my junior year of high school, so we don't know each other too well. By the time she entered the family, I didn't need another mother figure. So, we're just in this weird place of building an adult relationship together.

My dad wanted me to stay with him while I was in town to spend as much time with me as possible. She was all for it. They had a room for me and everything. It just felt weird for me, so we compromised and I'm staying in the apartment above the garage instead of in the main house with them.

Even still, I knock every time I go into the main house. It just feels respectful, and I never had the type of relationship with my dad where I just walked into his house. So, as I step up on his front porch, I knock. A moment later, he answers, shaking his head with a smile and stepping aside to allow me to come in.

"Shelly bought these nice summer place settings for the table that she has all set up and wants you to come see," he says, talking about his wife, who technically, I guess, is my stepmother.

So, I follow him to the back of the house where the kitchen and dining room are. Sure enough, there's the dining room table set up with these brightly colored floral placemats and fancy bright blue plates and cups. I would have loved this when I was a kid and even now, I have to admit it's kind of fun and a nice way to enjoy the summer.

"Oh, wow these are beautiful," I say as I take in everything down to the bright pink flamingo salt and pepper shakers.

"Aren't they? We were in Whitefish last week for your dad's doctor appointment and there was this store next door that I walked through to kill some time. I fell in love with these," she says, still fussing with something on the stove.

I turn to look at my dad to ask what was wrong with him and he simply shakes his head.

"It was my yearly appointment to keep my primary care doctor happy," he says, almost reading my mind.

"Oh, dear, yes sorry. I don't want to worry you. It was just his regular checkup appointment. As we get older, we have to keep up on those," Shelly laughs.

Shelly is only a year younger than my dad, so my dad tries to make comments about being too old for this, or that. Then she chimes in that they aren't too old for anything because she doesn't feel old.

"Have a seat at the table. Everything is ready," Shelly says as she turns and hands my dad a few things to put on the table.

"So, how are things going at the clinic?" Shelly asks as soon as we're all seated at the table and our plates were full of the chicken Caesar salad that she made with a side of pasta salad.

My dad's a sucker for a pasta salad, so Shelly makes it every chance that she can. Especially in the summer when they can use some of the ingredients from their garden.

"It's been going well. A lot of people come in during the day just to say hi and put a face to my name. We've only had a few pet owners who refused to see me because they don't know me. But with the number of people that are bringing their pets in just to have them checked out, I'm guessing we've more than made up for that business at the moment."

"Ace has been there just in case that guy was to come back?" Dad asks.

"Every day he's there before I get there, and he stays until I leave. Normally, he's just out in the parking lot keeping an eye on things, but if the weather's been bad and things are slow, he'll come inside and keep me company."

"He's a good guy, you know." My dad watches me for some kind of reaction, and I get the feeling that he's trying to lead into an entirely other conversation.

"Oh, he was nice when he was here the other day," Shelly says with a big smile on her face, but my dad instantly gets uncomfortable.

"When was he here? Why?" I ask, wondering how I missed it.

"He was here the other night when you ran into Whitefish to go pick up the supplies. He came to talk to me and then he had dinner with us," my dad says.

I had gone to pick up items for the people taking care of the cats. We couldn't get the shipment of milk delivered soon enough, and another vet allowed us to get some from them.

"Talk to you about what?" I ask as my dad tries to dance around the question.

"Oh, dear, I'm so sorry I shouldn't have said anything." Shelly rests a hand on my dad's arm.

"Nah, it's okay. I don't have anything to hide. He came over because he wanted to have my blessing to date you. He and I have known each other since he came to town, and with the club and everything, he just wanted to make sure that everything was on the up and up."

"He had no right to come here and bother you with this. What happens or doesn't happen between us is our business. It doesn't concern you." I start to get all riled up because I had already decided to see what Ace and I have because that type of connection just doesn't feel like something from which I can walk away.

"Well, I completely agree with all of that. I told him I'd be fine with you guys dating, but the ultimate decision is up to you. I'll support you in whatever you decide," my dad says.

I freeze, my brain going blank.

"Wait... what?" I sputter.

"Why is it a shock to you that I would support you in your decisions about your love life?" My dad asks the question with a look of concern on his face.

"Because of the promise that you had me make," I say, like it's the most obvious thing in the world.

My word means everything to me, so I don't make promises lightly. When I promised my dad not to date guys like him, motorcycle guys, and especially guys from any MC club he was in, I didn't make that promise frivolously. It's been on my mind ever since, and when I saw Ace's patch, I freaked out.

I talked myself down because with Ace it was supposed to just be a one-night stand, and I could forget about it. But as I'm learning, it's a small town, and he just kept showing up.

"What promise is that?" he asks.

I have to fight rolling my eyes. "When I promised you that I was never going to date a guy like you. A motorcycle guy."

It takes a moment, but then a hint of recognition crosses his face. "Oh, sweetheart, I never should have asked you to make that type of promise. I was in a bad place. The guys I used to run with weren't good people. But the Mustang Mountain Riders? They're one of the best groups of guys out there, and I would be ecstatic for you to date any one of them," my dad says softly.

I sit there, almost in shock, going over this new piece of information in my head. I know only a tiny piece of what type of person my dad used to be. My mom shielded me quite a bit, and I haven't asked my dad about any of it since we reconnected as adults. I'm honestly not sure if I want to, because that's his past, and I want to get to know him now.

"Ace is a really good guy, and for what it's worth, I think you should give him a chance. But that is your decision to make, and I will support you either way." My dad rests his hand on my arm.

Well, this changes everything.

I'M TENDING the bar when the door slams open and Everly stomps her way over to where I'm wiping down a table. It's clear as day she is mad about something, only I have no idea about what. I know she was having dinner with her dad earlier tonight and I wonder if something went wrong there.

"Is everything okay?" I ask hesitantly as I place an arm around her back and steer her towards my office, so we don't make a scene.

"You went and talked to my dad?" she says as she crosses her arms, putting as much space as she can between us in the small office at the back of the bar.

"Ahh. Yeah, it was the right thing to do," I tell her, still not sure why she's so angry about this.

"My dad and I don't exactly have the picture-perfect relationship. This is something that we should have talked about because getting my dad involved in my life should be my decision. You don't know the past that we have," she says, rambling a bit.

"In all fairness, I had a relationship with your dad before you came into town. He's been like a mentor to me since I joined the club. I felt like I at least needed to come clean with him because going behind his back didn't seem like the right thing to do."

"Then, at the very least, I should have been there when you two had a talk. But in all reality, it should have been me going and talking to my dad about us, not you. If you needed to talk to him that's fine, but you should have done it after I talked to him. Which is why you and I should have had this conversation first." She raises her voice and my gut twists.

She slumps back against the wall like all the fight in her is gone. Though I can still tell that even reaching out to comfort her would be the wrong thing right now. Her arms are tightly crossed against her chest, and there's still a fire in her eye saying she's not done fighting.

I'm not sure how to make her understand why I did what I did, but I'm sure as hell going to try my best.

"I was never going to be okay with putting that talk on your shoulders. You are my woman, and you have to let me take care of you. That's how I show you I care. I'm not great at all the mushy, gushy romantic stuff, but I will always take care of you."

"That's not who I am. You have to let me be independent, too."

"I don't know if I can do that. I'm always going to be there to take care of you, sweetheart."

"Ugh, you aren't listening," she says. Without another word, she turns around and leaves the bar, just as angry as when she walked in.

While I know I should go after her and say something to fix this, only I have no idea what to say or how to make it better. I never thought I'd lose her over the fact that I wanted to take care of her. When I take a step towards the door, still with no idea what I'm going to say, a familiar voice speaks out from the seat at the end of the bar.

"From experience, you have got to let her cool off a little bit." I turn to find Noah sitting there alone.

The dim light hides the scars on his face, but the ones on his arm are clear as day in his short-sleeve shirt. Noah owns and runs the rehabilitation center I was in after I was hurt in the line of duty. He and his wife, Lexi, run the place, and it was so much better than recovering in the hospital.

He's also the last person I expect to see in my bar. Especially after the way we left things. With one more glance towards the door, knowing that Everly is probably long down the road by now, I sigh and step behind the bar to face my past.

"What are you doing here?" I ask Noah, not even bothering to see if he wants a drink. Because I'm not sure if I want to hear what he has to say or not.

"Well, it took a little bit to track you down, but you didn't think I was just going to let it go, did you?"

"Honestly yeah, I did. What was the point in tracking me down?"

"Because I have yet to have a patient not finish his treatment, and I'm not going to start now. We've set everybody up with a job, a school, and a place to live. I wanted to make sure you had all that."

"Well, thanks to my uncle I do. He left me this bar, his cabin, and enough money to live comfortably. I've even made some friends here," I tell him, hoping to get him off my back.

"And how long before you run away from them, too?"

"I don't run away. I've been abandoned over and over, first by my father and my grandparents and most recently by the military. Even you and your fancy rehab abandoned me when I needed you most."

"How were we going to abandon you? What part of me flying thousands of miles out here says we abandoned you?" Noah asks calmly, but the confusion is written all over his face.

"You were getting ready to discharge me when I wasn't ready. I had nothing, and if my uncle's will hadn't come in just a few weeks before, I really would have had nothing."

"So, you eavesdropped on part of a conversation, and instead of getting the full story, you up and left?"

"What more could there be to the story?" I say, handing one of the regulars a refill on his beer.

"What we said was you were ready for discharge, which means you start working with one of our transition specialists. Then we make sure you have a job and a place to stay. We set you up with doctors and ensure you have people in your corner and a game plan of what you're going to do. We don't just throw you back into the cold because your treatments are done."

"You don't know what it's like out here in the real world when you carry scars from your previous life. It's not that easy." I shake my head. I don't know how to make him understand what I needed at that point was a transition to the civilian world.

Noah may have scars, but he lives in this pretty little bubble surrounded by people with scars like him or worse. Yet things just don't work that way out here. As long as Everly was okay with them, no one else's opinion matters. Well, that was before she walked out on me today.

"*I don't know what it's like?* Dude, have you seen me? When I had my accident, I was engaged to a girl, and we had planned to get married after deployment. She walked in, saw my scars, told me how ugly I was and that I was going to ruin her wedding photos, and left. Lexi had to drag me kicking and screaming back to the land of the living. The first time she took me out in public, I was terrified. People stared. Hell, they still stare. I can't even begin to count how many stares and whispered comments I got between getting on the plane in Atlanta and getting off the plane here. I get it. At least you can cover yours up with a shirt."

His words make him sound irritated, but his tone is

almost whimsical. He's smiling like this conversation amuses him.

But it does make me think of him flying here, and all the people he had to encounter to do so.

"I didn't come here to argue. I came here to make sure that you were okay." He sets a manila envelope on the bar and slides it toward me.

"What's this?" I ask, not even picking it up.

"The paperwork you would have been given if you had stuck around. It's tailor-made to whatever location where you're going to end up. So yours is set for here in Montana. It lists your VA benefits, your coverage, contacts, and support groups. And it reminds you that you're always welcome at Oakside. We won't abandon you because you're family. If you ever need to talk to me, or want to catch up, I'm here. If you need help to plan a wedding, event, or proposal, Lexi is more than happy to help. We aren't going anywhere, and I'm always just a phone call away. My number is in that pack, too."

Picking it up with shaky hands, I open it. Sure enough, everything he said is in there, colored pamphlets, paperwork, and business cards.

"Just about the only thing I can't help you with is your girl there. I don't know what happened, but she sounded pissed, and I barely keep it together when I make Lexi mad. I'm not the one to take advice from."

"Got some time? I'll tell you all about it."

"I've got plenty of time," he says with a smile.

I pour him a drink, making sure everyone else is

taken care of before I launch into the story of how Everly and I met.

Noah has always been one of those people that I just seem at ease around. Knowing that he's still going to be in my life, it changes things.

I'm setting down roots here in Mustang Mountain. For the first time in my life, I'm starting to feel like I truly belong.

That was until Everly walked out that door tonight.

THIS MORNING, I'm at the clinic cleaning up after surgery. We aren't seeing patients today, so I let the staff go home to have some time with their families. So, when the front door slams shut, I jump. I thought I locked that damn door.

Maybe it's someone bringing in an injured animal, so I turn to head towards the front door.

"Everly? You really should be locking that door when you're here alone." Ace's growly voice fills the room before I'm able to take a step.

"What are you doing here?" I ask, because he is probably the last person I expected to see today.

He looks around the clinic and then he looks at me like he needs to make sure I'm okay. His face is soft, almost sad, and he doesn't look like he slept.

"I came to apologize. You were right. It was your family, and I should have let you decide how to deal with talking to your dad. I'm sorry I wasn't able to put myself in your shoes. But I don't have family like you do, and if you'd been able to go and talk to my mom, I would have been thrilled."

"Ace I—"

"Let me finish, please. I know I'll regret it for the rest of my life if I don't get this out and at least try."

I nod, unsure where he's going with this, but it seems important to him.

"It's instinct to want to protect you, and I can't describe it any other way other than the need to safeguard and take care of you. But if you need to be more independent, then I'll learn how to allow you to be more independent. Just please give me another chance."

"What do you mean, another chance? We had a fight. That's what couples do. You can't go off thinking every time we fight that I'm leaving you." I shake my head and step into his arms.

I was angry, yes, but the thought of ending things with him never once crossed my mind. My dad stating that he was a good guy just gave me more confidence to take a chance on us... to give us a try.

"What? But you..." He shakes his head and takes a deep breath before looking back at me and trying again. "When you left the bar last night you were so mad, I thought that was it, that we were done."

"I don't want us to be done. Do you?" I ask, needing to know for sure that we're on the same page.

"Fuck no I don't. I don't ever want to be done with

you," he says before closing the space between us and pulling me into his arms.

He rests his head on top of mine as I wrap my arms around him. We stand there for a minute holding each other and it feels so good and right to be in his arms.

"I spent all night trying to figure out how we can even be together. You seem so adamant about going back to Denver, and I hate big cities. If I have to, I'll follow you. We'll make it work," he says, kissing the top of my head.

My heart races knowing that he would give up his life here just to be with me. He's finally putting down roots. He feels at home here, and I know how big of a deal that is.

"I can't ask you to do that," I say, pulling away just enough so I can look into his eyes.

"You didn't ask." He leans down to kiss me.

Our lips touch for just a moment before I pull back.

"No, I know what it means for you to be here."

He looks into my eyes searching for the truth before running a hand through my hair.

"I can talk to Mr. Thomas about you staying on as a vet here at his clinic. It's time for that old man to retire anyway from what everyone's been saying," he says.

I just shake my head. I've always known the emotion of my heart sinking, but I can honestly say up until this moment I've never seen that moment happen with someone else. But when I shake my head no, I can almost feel Ace's heart sink. Also, it's written all over his face.

"This is why you have to let me be independent and you have to let me handle things on my own. You've already had a conversation with Mr. Thomas. You're right, he is ready to retire. But he wasn't about to leave the town without a small animal vet, because he knows Asher can't take on his clientele. So, I'm going to work alongside him for the next few months with the intent of taking over for him."

He stands there in shock, as if he's waiting for a punchline. Then he pulls me impossibly closer to him.

"You're serious? You're going to stay?" he asks like he's trying not to be too hopeful.

"Yes, Mustang Mountain has kind of grown on me, and I'd like to have the time to get to know my dad. I am in zero hurry to run back to Denver."

A huge smile lights up his face, and in the blink of an eye, he drops to the floor. For a brief second, I think something's wrong until I realize that he didn't drop to the floor, he dropped to one knee.

In his hand is the most gorgeous ring I've ever seen. It has an antique setting, and I know there's no way he walked into a jewelry shop and just picked this up.

"I knew that first night there was something special about you. We may have had an unconventional start, but the more I get to know you, the more I know I need you in my life. This ring is the one thing my mother left me. It belonged to her grandmother, and it's been passed down on the female side of the family. But since she only had me, it was given to me with the intention of it going to my future wife. I love you, and that's why I'm hoping you will make me the happiest man in the world and agree to become my wife," he says, slightly awkwardly and shyly.

This is a completely different side of him, one I haven't seen before, and one I kind of hope to see again.

"Yes, of course I will! I love you too!" I say.

Then he slips the ring onto my finger and pulls me into his arms.

"As much as I would like to make love to you again here in this office, I'd like to have you in my bed. Our bed," he corrects himself, and I smile as I let him drag me out the door.

Ace

I WANTED to tell her dad about the engagement right away. He knew it was coming because we talked about it at the dinner we had together. He told me that he would be ecstatic if and when it happened.

But learning from past mistakes, I let Everly take the lead. She wanted to head to my place and stay in our little bubble for a few days, which we did.

When we finally told her dad, he was so happy he insisted on throwing a very casual engagement party at the club in the form of a barbecue. We also did a video call with her mom to tell her the news. Though her mom was more shocked than excited. I guess she didn't see it coming because she and Everly hadn't talked as much since she came to Mustang Mountain.

Now that her mom's had time to get used to the idea, she seems excited to help plan the wedding.

First, we have an engagement party at the MC club to attend. Everly insists on taking the bike. Ever since our first ride on it where she was hesitant, she's been wanting to ride it more and more. She says she understands why I enjoy riding it so much and the freedom I feel with the wind in my face.

I tell her I plan to marry her before the end of the year so she can go with me on the first ride next year. Each year the club makes a huge event out of the first ride of the season, usually through Glacier National Park. After a long hard winter, it's an event we all look forward to. Only members and their wives are allowed. No girlfriends or fiancées.

She likes the idea of getting married before the end of the year, and I tell her there are just a few people I want to invite from out of town. Of course we'll invite all my MC brothers. Otherwise, whatever she wants for the wedding is perfectly fine with me.

When we get to the club, there are already a bunch of people there. I can hear some kids laughing and having a good time in the side yard of the club.

With Everly's hand in mine, we walk into the club, and the sight that greets me is one I can honestly say I never expected to see. Not only are the guys there with their girls, but many of the men also have one of the kittens they rescued from Everly and me. The other guys are playing with them. Cat toys are scattered around the room as well. These cats are just a few weeks old and just starting to walk.

"What are you doing here?" Everly's voice grabs my attention as two men walk up to her, and I'm instantly on guard.

"You didn't think you could announce your engagement and get away with not introducing us to your fiancé did you, little sis?" The slightly taller one says.

It takes me a minute to I realize these are her brothers.

They both wrap her up in a big hug before turning to me.

"This is Ace. Ace, this is my oldest brother Nolan and my youngest brother Leo."

"Still older than you!" Leo says with a huge grin on his face.

"I can't believe you guys are here," she says, hugging them again.

"Well, your dad called us up and told us about the engagement party. We weren't going to pass up a reason to come back to Mustang Mountain. We miss this place," Nolan says.

"Is Mom here?" she asks, looking around. Even I can hear the hint of hope in her voice.

"No, I don't think she'll be coming back to Mustang Mountain unless you plan on getting married here. Even then, I think she'd only be in town long enough for the ceremony and that will be it. She told me to tell you she plans on throwing you an engagement party in Denver though," Nolan says.

"Well, I do plan on getting married here in Mustang Mountain. I don't think I can picture any place more beautiful." Everly gives me a smile.

Her dad walks up then and starts introducing us to people. I already know almost everyone here, but as he's introducing them to his daughter, he doesn't miss a chance to introduce me as his soon-to-be son-in-law. Judging by the smile on his face, he is so proud of that fact.

Several conversations later, Everly is talking to one of the guy's wives about an issue with their senior dog. I'm standing there with my arm around her waist just looking around, and I realize that I finally have the family I've been chasing all these years.

The best part of all is that Everly fits right in.

EPILOGUE
SHAW

I'D JUST POPPED the cap off a bottle of beer and was about to start working on a classic bike I'd picked up at an auction when the sound of metal scraping over gravel came from my drive. Seemed odd since I hadn't heard anyone pull in.

I set the beer on my workbench and headed out front to see what the hell was going on.

"What the fuck?" My eyes had to be playing tricks on me. I squinted at my Harley sitting on its side in the middle of the gravel drive. I hadn't even had a sip of my beer yet, but I could have sworn there was a fucking goat standing next to my bike.

It lifted its head and looked up at me. Big buggy blue eyes watched me while its jaw slowly moved back and forth. I'd seen strange things happen in Mustang Mountain, but as far as I knew, no one around here had ever seen a goat materialize out of thin air.

I squeezed my eyes shut, thinking maybe I'd been

putting in too many hours at the garage. Mack was always joking that the fumes were going to go to my head. But when I blinked my eyes open, the damn goat was still standing there.

"Where the hell did you come from?" I moved closer, trying not to scrape my work boots against the rocks and scare it away.

Either I'd hallucinated the dumbest goat in the world, or the creature in front of me was used to being around people. The damn animal didn't move an inch while I approached, except to swish its hairy chin from side to side while grinding something between its teeth.

I wondered what it was chewing on. Then it bent down and ripped off a piece of the seat of my bike. The strip of black leather hung there for a moment before the goat slurped it into its mouth like a wide piece of spaghetti.

"Are you fucking kidding me?" I charged, ready to defend my bike with my life.

The goat lowered its head slightly, but didn't seem threatened. I'd almost reached it when a woman's voice came from the other side of the drive.

"There you are! Scapegoat, get over here!" She came through the trees, and I blinked to clear my vision again. My MC brothers were never going to stop giving me shit if they found out what kind of mindfuck I had going on tonight.

I knew everyone who lived on this remote side of the mountain. My closest neighbor was over half a mile away, and there was only one other cabin higher up the mountain before the road ended. The Sugarman place had been empty for about six months, ever since the old man took an extended vacation to visit his daughter out in North Carolina.

So where the hell did the curvy brunette and her goat sidekick come from?

Twigs and pine needles stuck out of her long brown hair, making her look like some sort of forest fairy. A smudge of dirt stretched across one cheek. When she turned my way, the warmth in her amber eyes made me stop in my tracks.

"You must be my new neighbor. Hi, I'm Eden." She thrust her hand forward. Dozens of bracelets stacked up her forearm. Some intricate design covered the back of her hand, almost like a tattoo, though I'd never seen anything quite like it. She had on a sheer, flowy top with a tank underneath that showed off some amazing curves. The kind of curves my palms itched to slide over and my fingers ached to grab onto.

Her gorgeous eyes drew me in. Flecks of gold sparkled in the depths of her irises. I even took a step closer before I pulled myself out of the weird spell she must have cast over me.

"Neighbor?" I crossed my arms over my chest, making it pretty clear I wasn't feeling very neighborly about her goat snacking on a custom leather seat that cost me over five-hundred bucks. I'd deal with that in a minute. First, I needed to find out who she was and what the fuck she was doing in my driveway. "You lost, sweetheart?"

Dark lashes fluttered against her cheeks before she tilted her head back to meet my gaze. I got the sense she had a backbone of steel under her soft exterior. "The only thing lost around here was Scapegoat. I just moved in up the road. Eden Sugarman. You've got a lot of negative energy in your aura. I can help you release that if you'd like."

I squinted down at her. "What are you, some kind of witch?"

Her laugh was like the sound of a wind chime in the breeze, almost musical.

"Wait, did you say Sugarman?"

"That's right. My grandfather owned the place up the road." She hooked her thumb and gestured over her shoulder. "He passed away a few months ago and left me this place, so here I am."

"No." I shook my head. "That can't be right."

"He talked about Mustang Mountain all the time. Listening to him go on about it, I knew it would be the perfect spot for me and my little brood." She wrapped her fingers around a collar I hadn't noticed on the goat's neck.

"But Leroy and I had an understanding. He was going to sell me his place, along with the building he owns in town, once I had the cash saved up for a down payment." We'd talked about it on more than one occasion. He was ready to leave Mustang Mountain, but said he'd wait until I was ready to buy him out.

Eden cocked her head. "My grandfather never said anything to me about that."

"Why would he?" I funneled both hands through my hair as I felt my future slipping through my fingers. "Based on what he told me, it didn't sound like he was very close to his family."

Eden's eyes narrowed slightly. "There are always two sides to every story."

"So, what? You're just moving in and that's that? I had plans for that cabin and the land around it. Not to mention what I intended to do with the building in town." I'd spent the last five years scrimping and saving so I could afford Sugarman's asking price, and I was so close to having enough for a down payment, I could taste it. Now this forest nymph was going to swoop in and take it all away with one wave of her bangly, jangly arm?

"That's the thing about plans, neighbor,"--she tugged the goat away from my bike and toward the break in the trees where she'd first stumbled through— "they change. I'm sorry about your motorcycle. I'll stop by tomorrow and see if I can patch it up for you."

"Patch it up? That's a five-hundred dollar custom leather seat." My stomach churned. Heat raced across my chest and straight up my neck to flood my face. I hadn't been this riled up in a long, damn time.

"Anger issues, too, it seems. We'll have to work on that. I'll bring some chamomile tea. Maybe some of my homemade lavender goat milk soap too."

Tea? Soap? Who the fuck did she think she was? I was about to follow her through the break in the trees when my phone rang. My younger brother Caden's number lit up the screen.

"Yeah?" My voice came out rougher than I intended, thanks to my run-in with Leroy's granddaughter. This day had taken a nosedive, and I didn't know how it could get any worse.

"Hey, I just stopped in to grab a pizza before heading home and thought you'd want to know. There's a flyer with your picture on it saying you're the mountain man of the month for September."

"What?" Damn Ruby Nelson. She'd been working her way through the mountain men on Mustang Mountain, convinced all of us were just waiting for the right woman to show up in our lives so we could settle down.

"You want me to rip it off the board?" Caden asked.

I glanced at my bike, still laying on its side. There was no way I'd ride it into town with the seat looking like it did and I'd let Caden borrow my truck since I had his up on the rack at the garage.

"Yeah, and if you see Ruby, tell her I'll be stopping in at the merc on my way to the garage in the morning. There's no fucking way I'm going to let her fuck around with my life."

"I'll tell her, bro." Caden disconnected.

Didn't I have enough problems in my life without having to deal with Ruby and the curvy brunette? Women... they'd never brought me anything but trouble. The sooner I got both Ruby and my new neighbor out of my life, the better off I'd be.

WANT MORE ACE AND EVERLY? **Sign up for our newsletter** and get the free bonus scene here: https://www.matchofthemonthbooks.com/Ace-Bonus

Make sure to grab Shaw's story in **September is for Shaw**. Then Owen's story is next in **October is for Owen**!

September is for Shaw: https://matchofthe monthbooks.com/september-shaw

October is for Owen: https://www. matchofthemonthbooks.com/October-Owen

MOUNTAIN MEN OF MUSTANG MOUNTAIN

Welcome to Mustang Mountain where love runs as wild as the free-spirited horses who roam the hillsides. Framed by rivers, lakes, and breathtaking mountains, it's also the place the Mountain Men of Mustang Mountain call home. They might be rugged and reclusive, but they'll risk their hearts for the curvy girls they love.

To learn more about the Mountain Men of Mustang Mountain, visit our website (https://www.matchofthe monthbooks.com/) join our newsletter here (http://subscribepage.io/MatchOfTheMonth) or follow our Patreon for extra bonus content here (https://www.patreon.com/MatchOfTheMonth)

January is for Jackson - https://www.matchofthe monthbooks.com/January-Jackson

February is for Ford - https://www.matchofthe
monthbooks.com/February-Ford

March is for Miles - https://www.matchofthemon
thbooks.com/March-Miles

April is for Asher - https://www.matchofthemonth
books.com/April-Asher

May is for Mack - https://www.matchofthemonth
books.com/May-Mack

June is for Jensen - https://www.matchofthemonth
books.com/June-Jensen

July is for Jonas - https://www.matchofthemonth
books.com/July-Jonas

August is for Ace - https://www.matchofthemonth
books.com/AceAugust

September is for Shaw - https://www.matchofthe
monthbooks.com/September-Shaw

October is for Owen - https://www.matchofthe
monthbooks.com/October-Owen

November is for Nate - https://www.matchofthe
monthbooks.com/November-Nate

December is for Dean -
https://www.matchofthemonthbooks.com/December-Dean

ACKNOWLEDGMENTS

A huge, heartfelt thanks goes to everyone who's supported us in our writing, especially our HUSSIES of Mountain Men of Mustang Mountain patrons:

Jackie Ziegler

To learn more about the Mountain Men of Mustang Mountain on Patreon, visit us here: https://www.patreon.com/MatchOfTheMonth

OTHER BOOKS BY KACI ROSE

April is for Asher – Asher and Jenna

June is for Jensen - Jensen and Courtney

August is for Ace - Ace and Everly

Club Red – Short Stories

Daddy's Dare – Knox and Summer

Sold to my Ex's Dad - Evan and Jana

Jingling His Bells – Zion and Emma

Club Red: Chicago

Elusive Dom

Forbidden Dom

Chasing the Sun Duet

Sunrise – Kade and Lin

Sunset – Jasper and Brynn

Rock Stars of Nashville

She's Still The One – Dallas and Austin

Standalone Books

Texting Titan - Denver and Avery

Accidental Sugar Daddy – Owen and Ellie

Stay With Me Now – David and Ivy

Midnight Rose - Ruby and Orlando

Committed Cowboy – Whiskey Run Cowboys

Stalking His Obsession - Dakota and Grant

Falling in Love on Route 66 - Weston and Rory

Billionaire's Marigold - Mari and Dalton

A Baby for Her Best Friend – Nick and Summer

CONNECT WITH KACI ROSE

Website
Facebook
Kaci Rose Reader's Facebook Group
TikTok
Instagram
Twitter
Goodreads
Book Bub
Join Kaci Rose's VIP List (Newsletter)

ABOUT KACI ROSE

Kaci Rose writes steamy contemporary romance mostly set in small towns. She grew up in Florida but longs for the mountains over the beach.

She is a mom to 5 kids, a dog who is scared of his own shadow, and a puppy who's actively destroying her house.

She also writes steamy cowboy romance as Kaci M. Rose.

PLEASE LEAVE A REVIEW!

I love to hear from my readers! Please **head over to your favorite store and leave a review** of what you thought of this book!

Made in the USA
Columbia, SC
23 September 2024

42131098R00059